Zombies

by Janet Perry and Victor Gentle

Dedicated to Atom Paul, who serves a range of powerful cures to his zombie-like customers (for example, the authors) from the shrine of his coffeehouse, Brewed Awakenings, in Milwaukee, Wisconsin

Gareth Stevens Publishing
MILWAUKEE

For a free color catalog describing Gareth Stevens' list of high-quality books and multimedia programs, call 1-800-542-2595 (USA) or 1-800-461-9120 (Canada). Gareth Stevens Publishing's Fax: (414) 225-0377.

Library of Congress Cataloging-in-Publication Data

Perry, Janet, 1960-
    Zombies / by Janet Perry and Victor Gentle.
       p. cm. — (Monsters: an imagination library series)
     Includes bibliographical references (p. 22) and index.
     Summary: Discusses zombies, the walking dead or near-dead,
bodies without souls, in fact and fiction, and such related
phenomena as golems and animated mummies.
     ISBN 0-8368-2443-1 (lib. bdg.)
     1. Zombies—Juvenile literature. [1. Zombies.] I. Gentle, Victor.
II. Title. III. Series: Perry, Janet, 1960- Monsters.
GR830.Z65P47   1999
398'.45—dc21   99-22510

First published in 1999 by
Gareth Stevens Publishing
1555 North RiverCenter Drive, Suite 201
Milwaukee, WI 53212 USA

Text: Janet Perry and Victor Gentle
Page layout: Janet Perry, Victor Gentle, and Helene Feider
Cover design: Joel Bucaro and Helene Feider
Series editor: Patricia Lantier-Sampon
Editorial assistant: Diane Laska

Photo credits: Cover, pp. 5, 7, 13, 15, 17, 19, 21 © Photofest; p. 9 © 1998 Barbara Bussell/Network Aspen; p. 11 © Doug Perrine/Innerspace Visions

Printed in the United States of America

1 2 3 4 5 6 7 8 9 03 02 01 00 99

TABLE OF CONTENTS

Words that appear in the glossary are printed in **boldface**
type the first time they occur in the text.

IF THE DEAD WALK, YOU'D BETTER RUN!

What is operating this body walking toward you? The feet are shuffling as though the legs aren't attached. The arms are hanging like dead weights. The eyes stare straight through you.

This human body heading your way has lost the person that belongs in there.

All at once, you realize it's coming to *get* you. You know it's rude to leave without saying "hi," but it's suddenly time for you to be going . . . very quickly.

You didn't run fast enough. That's really too bad, because now you are about to become a zombie slave in a Cornish tin mine.

NO BRAIN, NO PAIN

What you have just read about is a zombie from a horror movie. In these movies, a witch doctor creates zombies by magically taking people's souls. Then he controls their minds and their actions. Usually, the zombies are innocent people in the wrong place at the wrong time.

In most movies, zombies cannot be killed because they are already dead. They lose pieces of their bodies when they are hit, sliced, or shot. They feel no pain and are incredibly strong.

Real zombies are not like this.

This witch doctor is dressed to kill a soul in the movie *The Serpent and the Rainbow*. The costume is designed to make the zombie believe it "died" by being shot.

VOODOO DEATH AND LIFE

So, are there real zombies? Yes! In real life, there is a religion called **voodoo**. Voodoo priests and priestesses are like doctors and judges. They play an important part in many people's lives in Brazil, Cuba, Haiti, Nigeria, and some other countries, too. Voodoo is also a religion in New Orleans, Louisiana, in the United States.

In voodoo, a zombie is a person who has gone through a ritual to release his or her troubled soul. The soul may have left, but the body is still alive. If a new soul is born into the empty person, then the body is healed from the damage of the soul that's been removed.

The woman with the red cloth on her head is a voodoo priestess. She is guiding a healing ritual in sacred mud.

BUGS, BEANS, BONES, AND BELIEF

Wade Davis is an American **ethnobotanist** (a scientist who studies the plants used by certain groups of people). He was curious about which plants are used in voodoo "zombie powder" (a dust that seems to cause the zombie death). He wrote about his adventures in the book *The Serpent and the Rainbow*.

Mr. Davis talked to oungan (priests) and manbo (priestesses). He found different recipes for the powder, but the most important "ingredient" turned out to be faith. No one can make, or become, a zombie unless he or she believes in voodoo.

Zombie powder can be made of beans, bones, herbs, insects, toads, and puffer fish poison. This puffer is pumping itself up to warn, "Don't eat me!"

ZOMBIE MOVIES: DEAD WRONG — RIGHT?

In the movie *The Serpent and the Rainbow*, a lot of things happen that were not in the book. The lead character is poisoned after he finds what is used in zombie powder. Then he is buried alive. Neither of these things really happened to Wade Davis.

All of the scary things in the movie are there just to make a fun monster movie. Don't believe what you see in zombie movies.

The book talks about real life. Mr. Davis *did meet* some people who had been zombies. He also learned a lot about the voodoo religion.

The movie poster shows voodoo **symbols.**
Crosses and a whitened face mark a zombie death.
The burning ship carries a soul that won't return.

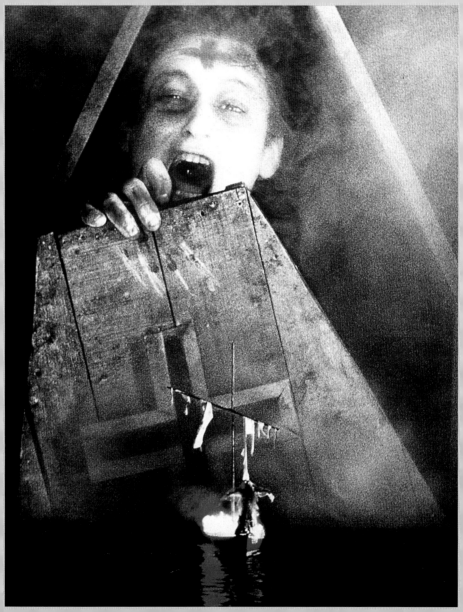

NOT REAL ZOMBIES, JUST MOVIE REEL ZOMBIES

In *Night of the Living Dead* (1968), dead people are brought back to life by **radiation**.

The Living Dead like to eat living humans. They walk and talk and lose their souls like zombies. They end up controlling the world just because they eat or infect the living.

They are not even close to being real zombies. According to Mr. Davis, voodoo priests may grind up dead people's bones to make zombie powder, but real zombies don't eat humans.

What is it that makes moviegoers want to see movies like this one? Why do people sometimes like to be scared — on purpose?

GOLEMS, GOOD AND GHASTLY

Other religions have traditions about beings without souls, beings created by holy people. One of these creatures is the **golem**.

In some Hebrew **traditions**, a **rabbi** can bring a golem to life using his deep knowledge of sacred texts. The golem must be created for pure religious purposes, or bad things happen.

In *Die Golem*, a German movie made in 1920, Rabbi Loew makes a golem to protect the Jews in Prague, in eastern Europe. However, Loew's servant uses the golem for evil, and things go very wrong.

In *Die Golem,* Loew's servant is in love with Loew's daughter. He misuses the golem to kidnap her and attack his rival. The golem goes out of control.

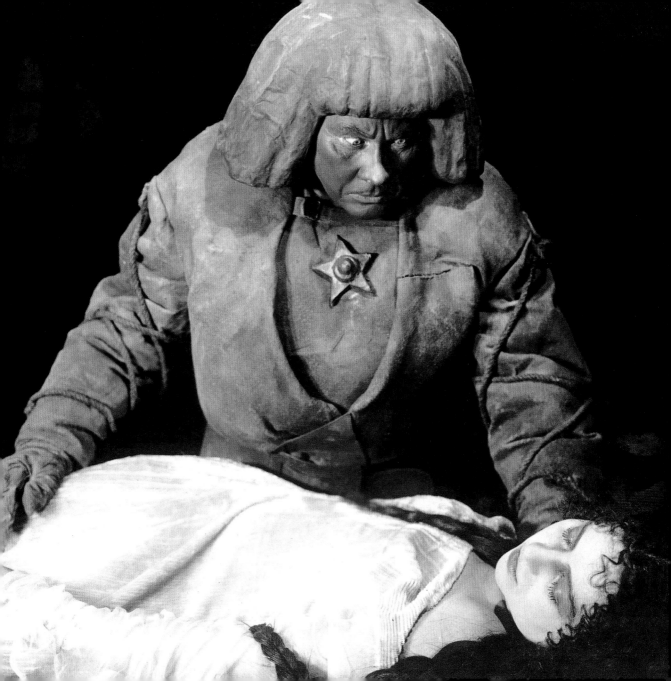

QUIT BLAMING MUMMY!

A **mummy** is a dead body, specially prepared and wrapped in bandages, and buried in an ancient Egyptian tomb.

In 1923, King Tutankhamen's tomb was opened by British **archaeologists** Howard Carter and Lord Carnarvon. False reports told of "the curse of the mummy's tomb." Anyone who entered the tomb was "doomed." When Carnarvon died of a mosquito bite, the curse seemed true. It was nonsense, but it was thrilling nonsense.

Mummies had absolutely nothing to do with the curse, but, in monster movies, they come to life to protect the tomb! Oh, those clever moviemakers!

Comedians Bud Abbott and Lou Costello are all wrapped up in their mummy's arms! They knew there was something funny about that curse . . . .

THE LIGHTS ARE ON, BUT NO ONE'S HOME

Mummies, golems, and zombies are all in some way bodies without souls. They are all based in serious religious beliefs about human life and death.

Monster movies are not scary unless it seems like they could be true. So, the movie writers build their monstrous stories around a few good facts and some real beliefs.

Enjoy the fun of monster movies, but remember that what you see in the movies is mostly just make-believe.

When you plant a corpse, you don't expect it to come up and bloom quite like this! Another spine-tingling scene from *The Serpent and the Rainbow*!

MORE TO READ, VIEW, AND LISTEN TO

Books (Nonfiction)

Bog Bodies: Mummies and Curious Corpses (True Stories).
  Natalie Jane Prior (Allen & Unwin)
The Encyclopedia of Monsters. Daniel Cohen (Dodd, Mead)
Haiti. Martin Hintz (Children's Press)
Haiti. Festivals of the World (series). Roseline NgCheong-Lum
  (Gareth Stevens)
Monsters (series). Janet Perry and Victor Gentle (Gareth Stevens)
Movie Monsters. Thomas G. Aylesworth (Lippincott)
Mummies (A Very Peculiar History). Nathaniel Harris (Franklin Watts)
Mummies, Tombs, and Treasure: Secrets of Ancient Egypt. Lila Perl
  (Houghton Mifflin)
Mummy. Jim Putnam (Eyewitness Books/Knopf)
Vampires, Zombies, and Monster Men. Daniel Farson (Doubleday)

Books (Activity)

The Ghosts, Witches, and Vampires Quiz Book. Arthur Liebman
  (Sterling Publishing)
Make-up Monsters. Marcia Lynn Cox (Grosset & Dunlap)
Monsters and Extraterrestrials. Draw, Model, and Paint (series).
  Isidro Sánchez (Gareth Stevens)

Books (Fiction)

Gideon and the Mummy Professor. Kathleen Karr (FSG)
Gods and Pharaohs from Egyptian Mythology. Geraldine Harris
  (Peter Bedrick Books)
The Golem. Isaac Bashevis Singer (FSG)
I Am the Mummy Heb-Nefert. Eve Bunting (Harcourt Brace)
Marcie and the Monster of the Bayou. Betty Hager (Zondervan)

Videos (Fiction)

The Cabinet of Dr. Caligari. (Timeless Video)
The Curse of the Mummy's Tomb. (Hammer Films/Warner)
The Golem. (Hollywood Select Video)
The Mummy. (Universal Studios)

WEB SITES

If you have your own computer and Internet access, great! If not, most libraries have Internet access. Go to your library and enter the word *museums* into the library's preferred search engine. See if you can find a museum web page that has exhibits on poisonous animals and plants, religions of the world, cultures of the world, the history of Haiti and New Orleans, Egyptology, and the history of the Jewish people. If any of these museums are close by, you can visit them in person!

The Internet changes every day, and web sites come and go. We believe the sites we recommend here are likely to last, and give the best and most appropriate links for our readers to pursue their interest in the folklore of zombies, Haitian culture, and related subjects.

www.ajkids.com

This is the junior *Ask Jeeves* site – a great research tool.
Some questions to *Ask Jeeves Kids*:
- *Where can I find information about voodoo spirits?*
- *Who eats puffer fish?*
- *What is a bouga frog?*

You can also just type in words or phrases with a "?" at the end, for example,
- *Golem?*
- *Voodoo religion?*
- *Zombies?*

www.mzoo.com

The Miniature Zoo has a special section of monsters and weird critters. Go to the site and click on the Quick Site Index to see pictures and links to many strange and unusual animals and insects – such as poisonous plants, snakes, toads, and fish!

www.yahooligans.com

This is the junior Yahoo! home page.
Click on one of the listed topics (such as Around the World, or Science and Nature) for more links. From Around the World, try Anthropology and Archaeology, Countries, Cultures, History, Languages, Mythology and Folklore, and Religion to find more sites about zombies, voodoo, Haitian culture, spirit worlds, mummies, Judaism, and whether people exist who actually eat poisonous animals and plants – and live to tell about it! From Science and Nature, you might try the Health and Safety link to Drugs and the History of Medicine. There, you can learn about how drugs are used and misused. You might also find fun facts about nontraditional medicine that really works! Search for more information by typing a word in the Yahooligans search engine.
Some words to try are: *botany, fish, frogs, golem, Haiti, mummies,* and *Tutankhamen.*

GLOSSARY

You can find these words on the pages listed. Reading a word in a sentence helps you understand it even better.

archaeologist (are-kee-AH-loh-jist) — a scientist who studies fossils from long ago 18

ethnobotanist (eth-know-BOTT-uh-nist) — a scientist who studies plants and the special ways they are used by different peoples 10

golem (GOH-lemm) — a human-like creature without a soul made by rabbis to protect Jewish communities 16, 20

mummy (MUH-mee) — a dead body that has been specially treated (to preserve it) and then wrapped in bandages 18, 20

rabbi (RAB-eye) — a Jewish leader 16

radiation (ray-dee-AI-shun) — energy that is sent through the air (or through space) in waves or rays 14

symbols (SIMM-buhls) — signs that stand for something else; for example, the "thumbs up" sign is a symbol that means "yes" or "I like it" 12

traditions (truh-DIH-shuns) — sets of ideas, beliefs, or customs passed on from one generation to the next 16

voodoo (VU-DU) — a religion that mixes ideas from Roman Catholicism and some African religions, including a belief in the ability of priests to remove a person's soul from his or her body. Voodoo is practiced in countries like Brazil, Cuba, Haiti, and Nigeria, and in New Orleans, Louisiana. The word *voodoo* comes from an African word meaning "god" or "spirit" 8, 10, 12, 14

INDEX